Xtreme Adventure

MOUNTAINEERING

BY S.L. HAMILTON

Visit us at
www.abdopublishing.com

Published by ABDO Publishing Company, PO Box 398166, Minneapolis, MN 55439.
Copyright ©2014 by Abdo Consulting Group, Inc. International copyrights reserved in all
countries. No part of this book may be reproduced in any form without written permission
from the publisher. A&D Xtreme™ is a trademark and logo of ABDO Publishing Company.

Printed in the United States of America, North Mankato, Minnesota.
102013
012014

Editor: John Hamilton
Graphic Design: Sue Hamilton
Cover Design: Sue Hamilton
Cover Photo: Thinkstock
Interior Photos: AlaskaStock-pgs 4-5, 6-7 & 14-15; Corbis-pgs 10-11, 24-25 & 28-29;
Dreamstime-pgs 20-21; Getty-pgs 8-9, 12-13, 18-19 & 22-23; Glow Images-pgs 16-17;
Kaj Sønnichsen-pgs 26-27; Thinkstock-pgs 1, 2-3, 28 (inset), 30-31 & 32.

ABDO Booklinks
Web sites about Xtreme Adventure are featured on our Book Links pages. These links are
routinely monitored and updated to provide the most current information available.
Web site: www.abdopublishing.com

Library of Congress Control Number: 2013946161

Cataloging-in-Publication Data

Hamilton, S.L.
 Mountaineering / S.L. Hamilton.
    p. cm. -- (Xtreme adventure)
Includes index.
ISBN 978-1-62403-212-7
1. Mountaineering--Juvenile literature.   2. Mountains--Recreational use--Juvenile literature.
I. Title.
796.52/2--dc23

                              2013946161

CONTENTS

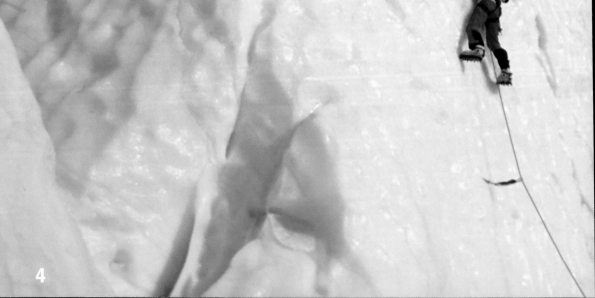

MOUNTAINEERING

Mountaineering is the sport of climbing mountains. Climbers pit themselves against the tallest or most difficult-to-reach peaks on the planet. They face freezing temperatures, bone-chilling winds, avalanches, slippery ice, and a lack of oxygen. A misplaced step can mean death.

Why do people seek out an adventure that could easily kill them? Famous mountaineer George Leigh Mallory said, "What we get from this adventure is just sheer joy." Climbers see wonders that others never will. A successful ascent provides the ultimate in extreme adventure.

XTREME FACT – Top mountaineers strive to climb the "Seven Summits." These are the highest mountain peaks on each of the seven continents: Everest, Aconcagua, McKinley, Kilimanjaro, Elbrus, Vinson, and Puncak Jaya.

CLIMBING GEAR

The most important gear begins with clothing that protects climbers in below-freezing conditions. Vital mountaineering equipment includes a climbing suit, boots, ski goggles, gloves, brimmed hat, helmet or headlamp with batteries, and scarf or face-and-neck gaiter. Multi-day treks require climbers to bring water, food, a first aid kit, oxygen canisters, a tent, and a sleeping bag.

Climbers need such equipment as ice axes, walking sticks, ropes, crampons, and a variety of carabiners, belay devices, nuts, and chocks. They also carry a map, compass, GPS unit, altimeter, and a handheld radio or cell phone.

XTREME FACT– Climbers carry cameras to photograph themselves as proof that they have reached a mountain's summit.

DANGERS

Mountaineering is a dangerous sport that requires concentration, common sense, and a respect for the weather. Many people die because they did not want to turn around. Long-time climbers know that it is "wiser to fail, than to die."

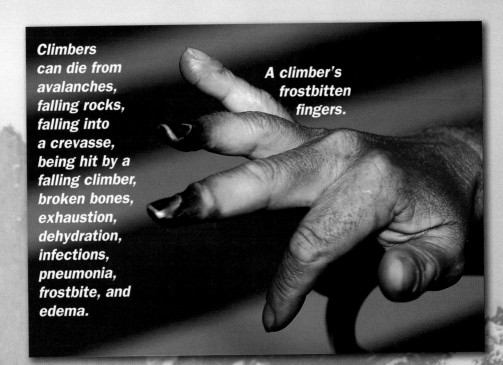

Climbers can die from avalanches, falling rocks, falling into a crevasse, being hit by a falling climber, broken bones, exhaustion, dehydration, infections, pneumonia, frostbite, and edema.

A climber's frostbitten fingers.

XTREME DEFINITION – The "death zone" is the point at about 26,000 feet (7,925 m) where there is not enough oxygen to sustain human life. Many climbers bring bottled oxygen. Others go up and come down quickly.

MOUNT EVEREST

Asia's Mount Everest is the world's highest peak. It rises approximately 29,035 feet (8,850 m) above sea level on the border between Nepal and Tibet. Everest is considered the ultimate mountain to climb. It has 15 routes available to reach the top. Each of them are dangerous.

To make the climb, people spend several days getting used to the altitude in base camp. Climbers go up the mountain over the course of several days. They rest in camps spaced out on the mountain. Adventurers must make the ascent in either May, June, or late September, when the winds are usually calmer. It is an expensive, dangerous trek, but one that every mountaineer dreams of doing.

XTREME FACT– As of 2011, more than 200 dead bodies are on Mount Everest. They are not removed because bringing bodies down off the mountain would likely cause additional deaths.

11

K-2

K-2 is the second-highest mountain on Earth after Mount Everest. It stands 28,251 feet (8,611 m). It is on the border between Pakistan and China. It is nicknamed "the Savage Mountain." Only 246 climbers to date have reached the top. Years can go by without anyone even trying.

XTREME FACT – One American climber died on K-2 in 1939 after being trapped by a storm for days at 25,000 feet (7,620 m). His remains and tent were discovered in 2002, having been carried to the base of the mountain during an avalanche.

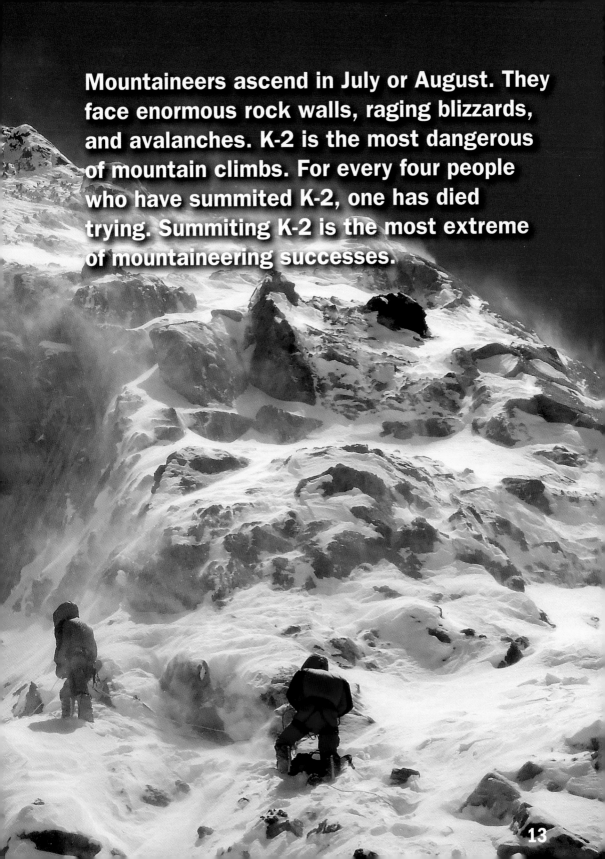

Mountaineers ascend in July or August. They face enormous rock walls, raging blizzards, and avalanches. K-2 is the most dangerous of mountain climbs. For every four people who have summited K-2, one has died trying. Summiting K-2 is the most extreme of mountaineering successes.

MOUNT McKINLEY

Alaska's Mount McKinley (also known as Denali or "The Great One") is the highest peak in North America. It reaches a height of 20,320 feet (6,194 m). The climbing season is best from May through July.

Mountaineers must first ski into the area, as aircraft cannot land near the mountain, except in emergencies. Most climbers go up McKinley over the course of about 20 days. Five camps are set up along the way. Climbers face deep crevasses, sharp buttresses, and ice-covered ridges.

XTREME FACT – *A climber attempting to summit McKinley in winter can be flash frozen. Extreme cold temperatures mixed with jet stream winds of 100+ mph (161 kph) can freeze a human in just minutes.*

ACONCAGUA

The highest mountain in South America is Aconcagua. It is 22,837 feet (6,961 m) tall. About 3,500 climbers a year go to Argentina to try to summit it. The Normal Route is a walk-up climb. However, the trail is covered with loose rocks called scree. An ice ax and crampons are often needed in certain sections of the trail.

XTREME FACT – Aconcagua is an extinct volcano. It is the highest mountain in the Western Hemisphere.

Climbers usually make the ascent from December to March. There are three camps up the mountain. Some people call Aconcagua an "easy" climb. However, the mountain can be deadly. Mountaineers face brutal winds, driving snow, avalanches, and extreme altitudes. There are no easy climbs in mountaineering.

KILIMANJARO

The tallest mountain in Africa is the flat-topped Kilimanjaro. It is located near Tanzania's northern border. The highest point is Uhuru Peak at about 19,341 feet (5,895 m) tall. Kilimanjaro is a walk-up climb with seven different routes.

XTREME FACT – More than half of Kilimanjaro's climbers get some form of acute mountain sickness.

Adventurers try to summit from December to February, when weather conditions are the clearest and warmest, or from July to September, when it is driest. Each year about 25,000 people try to reach Kilimanjaro's summit, which is known as the "roof of Africa."

MOUNT ELBRUS

Europe's highest mountain is Mount Elbrus. It is an extinct volcano found in Russia. The western summit is 18,510 feet (5,642 m), and the eastern summit is 18,442 feet (5,621 m). Climbing season is from May to September. It takes from four to seven days to acclimatize. As many as 100 people try to summit the mountain each day during the main climbing season.

XTREME FACT – In 1993, Outside magazine gave Mount Elbrus the award for having "the world's nastiest outhouse." It is perched over a cliff at 13,800 feet (4,206 m) up the mountain.

Station Garabashi, a climber's camp, sits at 12,467 feet (3,800 m) on Mount Elbrus.

Cable cars, chairlifts, and snowcats carry climbers as high as 15,092 feet (4,600 m) up Mount Elbrus. Because of this support, many inexperienced mountaineers expect an easy climb. But Mount Elbrus is one of the deadliest mountains in the world, with 15 to 30 deaths each season. Climbers face altitude sickness, fog, strong winds, and freezing conditions.

MOUNT VINSON

Mount Vinson in Antarctica was not summited until 1966. It was the last of the Seven Summits to be conquered. The mountain stands 16,050 feet (4,892 m) tall. Only about 1,400 climbers have attempted to summit Vinson. Climbing season is between December and February, when there are 24 hours of sunlight each day.

It takes about a week to acclimatize and climb Mount Vinson. Although calm, summer days may reach 20 degrees Fahrenheit (-7°C), mountaineers need glacier climbing gear to be prepared for possible raging winds and subzero temperatures.

XTREME FACT – Due to the difficulty in getting to Antarctica, a Mount Vinson climb may cost as much as $50,000.

PUNCAK JAYA

Puncak Jaya on Papua, New Guinea, is also called the Carstensz Pyramid. It is the highest peak in Oceania, standing 16,024 feet (4,884 m) tall. Its North Face Route is a difficult technical climb. Only about 100 people a year make the climb.

The best months for climbing Puncak Jaya are April to November. It is a steep, scree-filled vertical scramble using fixed ropes and technical gear. Climbers must also cross a number of wide gaps over several hundred-foot (30-m) drops.

XTREME FACT – To reach the base of Puncak Jaya, climbers must make a 62-mile (100-km) trek through the surrounding rainforest.

MOUNT KOSCIUSZKO

The highest mountain in Australia is Mount Kosciuszko. It is 7,310 feet (2,228 m) tall. Since it is on the Australian continent, some think that it should be the Seventh Summit, instead of Puncak Jaya on New Guinea.

XTREME FACT – The highest toilet in Australia is just below the peak of Mount Kosciuszko. A welcome sight!

Kosciuszko (Koz-ee-oz-ko) is a simple 5.5-mile (8.9-km) climb that only takes a few hours. As many as 100,000 people climb the trail to the summit each year. The best time to climb is from November through May, during Australia's summer. Sunglasses, water, and rain or cold-weather gear are the only equipment needed.

THE MATTERHORN

The Matterhorn is located in the Alps of Switzerland and Italy. It is one of the most popular mountains to climb in the world. Although not one of the Seven Summits, it is a "fourteener," reaching an elevation of 14,692 feet (4,478 meters).

During the summer months, 150 people per day attempt to summit the Matterhorn. It is one of the deadliest climbs, with fixed ropes, single-climber rock faces, ice, and snow. Mountaineers also must deal with inexperienced climbers who cause rock falls and avalanches.

XTREME FACT – About 12 people die each year while trying to summit the Matterhorn.

GLOSSARY

ACCLIMATIZE
To get used to lower oxygen levels at high altitudes.

ACUTE MOUNTAIN SICKNESS (AMS)
An illness caused by high altitudes and the resulting low amounts of oxygen in the atmosphere. Symptoms range from headaches to bleeding and disorientation.

ALTIMETER
A device that measures altitude.

BELAY DEVICE
A device that protects a roped climber from falling by using friction and a bent rope to slow a climber's speed.

CARABINER
A strong, metal link with a spring-loaded opening that climbers clip onto various pieces of safety equipment.

CRAMPON
A metal plate with sharp spikes that attaches to boots. Crampons are used by climbers and hikers to walk on ice without slipping.

CREVASSE
A deep crack in rock, ice, or the ground.

DEHYDRATION
Dangerous loss of water from the body. If a person does not get fluids, dehydration can cause death.

EDEMA

A life-threatening buildup of fluid in a body's cells that occurs at high altitudes. A person suffering from edema must be brought down to a lower altitude immediately or risk dying.

FROSTBITE

Damage to skin caused by severe cold.

GAITER

A tube-like collar worn to keep the neck and face warm.

OCEANIA

A region that includes Australia and nearby South Pacific islands, including Melanesia, Micronesia and Polynesia. Often referred to as a continent.

TECHNICAL CLIMBING

Difficult climbing that requires rope and other protective gear such as nuts and chocks.

INDEX